Jean read the letter before Randall mailed it. "I'll be your editor," she said.

They were the only ones sitting on the swings at recess. Randall wore a somewhat clean shirt. Jean read Randall's letter out loud.

> Dear Uncle Luke,
>   Will you come to Parents' Day next Thursday? Ma will be home sleeping from the pills or sick from the toothaches and can't come. All the parents come and talk to the teacher. They would let an uncle come.
>   Thank you very much.
>   Your nephew,
>   Randall

While Randall and Jean were working on the letter, some other kids gathered near the swings to listen. Paul Lunde offered a comment. "That sounds good, Randall. I hope your uncle comes. I'd like a look at his motorcycle."

Randall looked up surprised, and smiled.

RANDALL'S WALL

by Carol Fenner

A BANTAM SKYLARK BOOK
NEW YORK · TORONTO · LONDON · SYDNEY · AUCKLAND

*This edition contains the complete text
of the original hardcover edition.*
NOT ONE WORD HAS BEEN OMITTED.

RL 4, 008-012

RANDALL'S WALL

*A Bantam Skylark Book / published by arrangement with
Margaret K. McElderry Books, Macmillan Publishing Company*

PUBLISHING HISTORY
Macmillan edition published 1990
Bantam edition / October 1992

ISBN 0-553-48021-9

Published simultaneously in the United States and Canada

PRINTED IN THE UNITED STATES OF AMERICA

OPM   10 9 8 7 6 5 4 3 2

This book is for
brave Jean
at eleven years,
adventurer,
my friend in literature
and lunches,
my compatriot exploring
lakes
and bowling alleys.

Acknowledgments

My thanks to:

my sister, Faith King, and my niece Maria King, who heard the early stages of *Randall's Wall* and who, because of their training and intuitions, had valuable suggestions to make;

my mother, Esther Gerstenfeld, who listened, along with Faith, to serial readings of *Randall* at vacation breakfasts;

my niece Mary King, whose serious response to the manuscript strengthened my intent;

my young friend Jean Concannon, who heard *Randall* in fits and starts, and her pal Angela Bunce, who joined us for a reading of the bathing scene;

Ann Concannon, friend and colleague, for reading (and liking) the first full draft of *Randall's Wall*;

Jim Concannon, who remembered the "Lord Randal" poem and who supplied information that led me to many versions of that work;

Aurora Concannon, whose listening ear prompted

my discovery of the right name for Jean's older sister in *Randall's Wall*;

Jane Ratner, Barbara Zichterman, and Margaret Gaskell at the reference desk of Willard Library in Battle Creek, Michigan, who checked information for me with such knowledgeable enthusiasm;

my husband, Jay Williams, whose cognizance of present day political and societal labyrinths provided me with important facts;

my editor, Margaret K. McElderry, whose joy in *Randall's Wall* and whose honest and delicate touch made our work together on the manuscript a fructifying collaboration.

—*Carol Fenner*

RANDALL WAS DREAMING. HIS DESK WAS in back near the window and sometimes he looked out the window and dreamed. Sometimes he looked at the ceiling, dreaming. Sometimes he stared right through his desk top. He stared through the wood—through the inked names dug into the surface with ballpoint pens—through his own grimy hands and the dirt under his fingernails. And he found a much brighter place than a fifth-grade classroom at the John J. Meade Elementary School.

Sometimes Randall dreamed he was riding a motorcycle, one like his Uncle Luke's. His arms curved, reflecting the curve of the handlebars. His hands gripped. He kicked down on the starter. The motor chuckled and chugged. Then the 650 roared to life and Randall spun down the streets and toward the winding roads outside of town. He climbed hills and soared into the air at the top,

1

landing in a burst of speed, light as a paper plane, on the downward slope.

Randall did not hear the teacher. He didn't raise his hand. He did not talk to other kids in the class or smile secret smiles to a friend.

No one sat near Randall Lord at the back of the room. Even though his father had shaved his hair off and the head lice were gone, no one sat near Randall.

"He never takes a bath," whispered Tiffany Spizinski. "I wouldn't touch him with a ten-foot pole."

"He sleeps in his clothes and then comes to school," hissed Lynda Percherman.

"He stinks," said Paul Lunde simply. "He simply stinks."

"His family is probably very poor," said Jean Worth Neary, tucking her dark hair behind her ear.

Paul said, "Water is free."

Whenever the class lined up for lunch or recess or a special treat, all the fifth graders avoided standing near Randall Lord. He was always first or last in the line—*way* in front or *way* in back. Randall ate a free school lunch at a table all by himself in the crowded, noisy lunchroom.

On the school bus, everyone let Randall and his sister get on first. Then the rest of the kids crowded in, staying as far away as possible from the Lords.

Randall was drawing. Randall was drawing one of his dreams. He was making a deer on the lined paper. He drew the deer with light brown and dark brown markers, leaving little spots of white, sketching out long delicate legs through the printed blue lines. He colored in big glossy eyes.

It was the deer his Uncle Luke had shot last month when he took Randall hunting with him. Randall drew two stubby new antlers on the deer. He was making the deer come back to life. He was erasing the sound of the blasting bullets—the startled fear in the deer's eyes—the blood all over the fall leaves.

He drew a beautiful red heart on the deer's chest.

"Singapore," murmured Randall. "Your name is Singapore." It was the name of an island in the South China Sea that his class had been studying about.

The deer turned his young head toward Randall. The glossy eyes blinked.

"What a beautiful drawing!" exclaimed Ms. Birchwood, the teacher. Randall hadn't known she was standing behind his shoulder. "May I hang it in the hall?"

"No," said Randall. "He wants to stay here." Carefully he closed Singapore into his notebook. Ms. Birchwood looked thoughtful.

"Of course," she said.

It was Randall's oldest sister, Butterfly, who told him first about the wall. But Butterfly went away before he started school, before his father started staying away all the time, before Randall knew the wall for himself.

Victoria, his other sister, told him that Butterfly had gone to work for some crippled old man in a distant town. She had her own room with her very own bathroom at the old man's house. Victoria told him that Butterfly was going to high school in that other town.

Before he was in first grade, he wondered if Butterfly had taken her wall with her. He used to look for it around the house, the wall she said she took on the school bus and wore around herself all day. Victoria finally told him that it was invisible

and that you couldn't use someone else's wall anyway. Victoria had her own wall by that time. She
got it in first grade.

"Can you get out of it?" asked Randall, worried.

"You won't want to," said Victoria.

By the time he got into first grade himself, he
had forgotten what Butterfly looked like. He remembered her voice, gruff and sweet, and her bos-
oms, which were bigger than his ma's. He
remembered what Butterfly said about the wall.

"It's there," she said, "but it doesn't hurt. And
nothing can get you through it."

Two things happened to Randall in the middle of
first grade that gave him his own wall. One happened because of his curiosity. He had begun to
notice that he could make other children go away
just by getting close to them. Then he remembered
Butterfly's wall and he wondered if his own invisible wall was happening. He wondered if it was
happening to other children, too. But he watched
them and noticed that they seemed to be able to
get close to each other—to shove and grab and pat.

One little girl, however, and a couple of boys
seemed to have a wall. The girl interested Randall

most because she had a brace on one leg and she was always reading. She wore thick, rimless glasses that seemed about to crush her tiny nose. Overcome by his curiosity about her wall and about what she was reading so avidly, Randall was drawn close to her desk. She looked up. Her eyes, magnified by her glasses, widened even more. She began to scream, "Get away! Get away!"

Randall wondered if he'd stepped on her wall. After that, he avoided her and, although he longingly watched the wall-less children playing together, he never approached any of them again.

The other thing that built up Randall's wall was his drawing. Randall loved to draw. The bright array of crayons at school thrilled him. All that clean paper made him greedy. His first-grade teacher was a young, smiling woman whom, at first, he had adored. He drew picture after picture for her and earned several thank-you's. Gradually he noticed that Miss Grable did not smile as warmly at him as she did at some of the other kids and she never, never hugged him as she did little Tiffany or rosy Lynda or happy Paulie.

Randall's mother was pregnant with Toby, one of his little brothers, when Randall was in first grade. He was fascinated with the change in his mother's thin body, her ballooning stomach and breasts. While other children were drawing houses with spoke-trimmed suns above them, Randall drew his mother with the baby inside. He emphasized all the new things that the baby was doing to his mother's body—the stretched housedress, the shape of her new nipples. He drew a baby sitting inside his mother's stomach sucking his thumb.

Lynda Percherman, waggling by his desk, happened to glance at his drawing. She shrieked, "Miss Grable! Miss Grable! Randall's drawing dirty pictures!"

Randall grinned foolishly, glancing around him. He kept the grin pasted to his face when Miss Grable grabbed the drawings of his mother from him. "Why on earth did you draw *that*? What's wrong with you? You can sit in the hall until you decide you'll leave this kind of thing at home." Miss Grable crammed his pictures of his ma with the baby inside into her wastebasket.

Randall sat in the hall thinking about the drawings of his mother and wondering what had been wrong. Was it his mother? What was it Miss Grable wanted him to leave at home? He knew you had to leave your mother at home when you came to school. Was that the bad thing he'd done? Would he be able to sneak his pictures out of the wastebasket? Randall sat in the hall the rest of the afternoon. He began to wish for his wall. He began to dream of his wall and how no one could touch him through it.

Ms. Birchwood often said, laughing, that she would like to fail all of her fifth-grade class that year. She hated to see them leave her (except for Randall Lord). They were the smartest, most delightful students she'd ever had. The room was a rare collection of loud kids and quiet kids, of talent and brains, of pride and friendliness (except for Randall Lord). And they were a handsome bunch of kids, too. Here she had to include the Lord boy, for, filthy though he was, Randall was a handsome lad. His eyes were so blue they were almost purple. He had a strong, clear shape to his face. His shaved scalp only accented the fine outline of his head and Ms. Birchwood remembered that his hair, though lice ridden and uncombed, had been thick, a burned-butter color.

She never knew what to do about Randall. At the beginning of the school year, she had questioned the principal, Mr. Needem, about cleaning Randall up.

"It would not only help Randall," she said earnestly, "but the rest of the class could relax."

"Public Health was notified last year. They've visited the home, I'm sure," said Mr. Needem. He shrugged with a sigh. "The right to privacy is a law. Ties our hands. Besides, the school can't be responsible for bathing students, just like we aren't responsible for their religion." He looked pleased with his justification.

That's stupid reasoning, thought Ms. Birchwood. Aloud she said, "Well, you always say, Mr. Needem, that 'teaching is reaching' and I can't reach Randall Lord through all that dirt."

"Do the best you can," said Mr. Needem, a saying of his that always infuriated Ms. Birchwood since it seemed to imply that her "best" wasn't enough.

As for reaching Randall, Ms. Birchwood gave up. He wasn't at all stupid but he didn't listen in class. He seemed to read to himself well. But the few times she had him read out loud in front of the class he mumbled and stammered. It made the other students uncomfortable, too, when he got up to read. Tiffany Spizinski, whose desk was right in front, kept wiping her desk top with a tissue. So Ms. Birchwood avoided asking Randall to read aloud. It made everyone miserable, including Randall. Including me, she thought. The dirty boy was the only sour note in her beautiful class. She tried to ignore him except to make sure he didn't get too near the other children.

Randall was dreaming of hunting with his Uncle Luke. The early morning light was like golden ladders slanting through the bright autumn trees. His Uncle Luke was so quiet that he barely moved the bushes he hid in. Randall copied him, sharing the suspense, the secret.

Randall was dreaming. The young deer appeared, moving on dainty hooves, stepping carefully and listening. The light slanted across his back.

When Uncle Luke raised his gun, Randall called out, "Singapore!"

The deer bolted, ran away through the trees. The bullets sang like lost hornets. His uncle turned an angry eye on Randall. Randall stopped the dream, slapping his desk. *"No!"*

The classroom came into focus. Everyone was staring at him.

"I've never seen such filthy hands!" the fourth-grade teacher said to Ms. Birchwood. They were standing in the doorway of the fifth-grade classroom. "You could plant a garden under his nails!"

Ms. Birchwood nodded, shuddering. The fourth-grade teacher had had Randall last year.

"And the house! Looks bad from outside, but you should see the inside. It's disgusting. Randall sleeps with two brothers and an older sister, Victoria. The mother is practically useless—like a sleepwalker. The father is a real brute, runs roughshod over the whole family—when he's around, that is. Which isn't often."

"Needem said that the Public Health Department was taking care of things," inserted Ms. Birchwood.

"Oh, sure. Public Health has attempted some visits, but the father has run them off each time. I think the department has shelved the Lords. Way back on some dark shelf."

The fourth-grade teacher was a small woman with a round, serious face and round, serious hips.

11

Her face got rounder and more serious as she continued. "The oldest girl left some time ago. She's about eighteen or nineteen now. At least she tried to do some laundry once in a while, and she managed to keep herself neat. But you should see the sheets they sleep on. Gray and gummy, and Lord knows what crawling life lives there. Ever notice the bites on Randall's arms?"

Randall was listening. His old teacher and Ms. Birchwood were standing in the classroom doorway. He glanced at his bite-covered arms. Did something crawl in the sheets at night?

He looked at his own hands and really saw them as if for the first time. They were two shades darker than his dirty arms. There was dirt thick under his fingernails. His hands. Suddenly he hated his hands.

All through most of the afternoon, he sat on his hands. He did not draw. His daydreaming was fitful and ragged. He looked at the other students busy in their seats. Ms. Birchwood's voice was filled with words, like bees in a hive. She buzzed and hummed. The class hummed. Hands raised. Clean hands. Paul Lunde and Tiffany Spizinski whispered and giggled. Randall's own hands went to sleep. His head felt light; his stomach curled and uncurled.

Alone in the boys' bathroom he squirted the thin yellow liquid soap onto his hands. He soaped all the way up his arms. He scrubbed and scrubbed, hoping no one would come in and stare. The bathroom was out of paper towels. He stood by the sink and shook his arms.

Ms. Birchwood sat in the teachers' room, sipping Diet Coke. Outside it was snowing, a light November snow.

"Victoria Lord has been crying all morning," said a sixth-grade teacher sitting at a table next to her.

"About what? Victoria never cries," said Ms. Birchwood. "Those Lord children are stoic."

The sixth-grade teacher shook her head. "Victoria says her father will shave her head, too, if we send one more note home about the lice."

Ms. Birchwood groaned.

"Apparently, he chased her all around the house with some rusty pruning shears. Victoria's afraid to go home."

"What'd Needem say?" asked Ms. Birchwood.

"Oh, you know . . . that bit about religion."

"Will Victoria keep her lice then?" asked Ms. Birchwood.

"I gave her some special shampoo. But they don't have any water, you know," said the sixth-grade teacher.

Ms. Birchwood gasped. "No water!"

"Except for a rusty pump in the backyard. Margaret Semple visited their house last year—when Randall was in her class. Their inside water pipes burst two winters ago, and Daddy Lord is never home long enough to care. That outside pump water must be pretty cold."

Ms. Birchwood was silent, remembering the deer with the red heart.

When the weather was nice, Randall spent most of his time outdoors. He liked to get as far away from the house as he could. In the woods and fields beyond the house he climbed trees and spied on rabbits and foxes, often deer. Sometimes, whenever Victoria wasn't looking after their little brothers, they played "hide and shout" in the woods. It was a game their sister, Butterfly, had invented years ago. You only played it in the woods when it was getting dark and scary.

In winter, Randall climbed into the attic. Victoria was afraid of the attic, so he went alone. Most of the space was damp from leaks in the roof, but there was a place near the chimney that stayed dry and warm.

The attic used to be full of things stored by the family that had previously lived in the house. A long time ago his father had gone through the attic for anything useful. His mother had found a trunk of old clothes, which they had all used and worn out. Randall remembered a smiling Victoria in a green velvet coat that had come from the trunk along with a matching hat and a little muff to keep her hands warm.

Just boxes of old photographs and books remained. Randall had pushed the boxes close to the dry place near the chimney. He sometimes looked at the photographs of long-ago people. There was one fading shot of a family picnic. Everyone was smiling, sitting around an outdoor table on which he could identify a mouth-watering platter of fried chicken and two large, round pies. A lake glimmered in the background. Some of the children were wearing funny-looking bathing suits.

Randall liked to stand the picnic picture up against the box along with several of the other photos. He would sit beside them. "Pass the chicken," he would say. The long-ago people would smile at him from around the picnic table.

Randall looked at the books in the attic, too. Most of them were pretty dull but he found a good book called *Freckles*, about a one-armed boy in the Limberlost wilderness. He found several beautiful books filled with paintings and drawings by famous artists. When the light was good through the little window, he could spend all day looking at the books of paintings. If the light was weak, he had a picnic.

The stout woman from the Public Health Department knocked a second time at the door of the blighted old house. There was no doorknob, only a rag stuffed into the hole where the doorknob had been. A cold wind blew at her back. The snow, which had begun to fall thickly, whipped at her legs. Back in the driveway her car gave off a comforting mumble and her co-worker, a large bearded fellow, kept wiping the steamy passenger window so he could check on her. That was comforting, too.

On her last visit here several months ago that dreadful Tom Lord had snarled at her in the most abusive language she'd ever heard. His eyes were so furious and such a terrible force had emanated from his body that she had backed off feeling physically threatened. "Like he'd had a club in his hands," she told fellow workers later.

Well, he wasn't going to threaten her now. She felt brave and determined and *right*. Besides, she had the bearded "Rambo" Martin in the car.

Except for the fact that smoke had been coming from the chimney when they drove up, the house appeared deserted. She stepped back from the door to look again at the chimney. Snow was melting on most of the tumbling roof. Only an area near the chimney seemed to be airtight enough to hold the snow without melting it.

She gave a start. For an instant, behind the whirling flakes, she thought she'd glimpsed a face at the attic window. It wasn't there now. This place gave her the creeps.

The snow was fast obliterating the driveway and the stout woman from Public Health gave one last half-hearted knock at the door. Still no response.

Relieved, and righteous over her efforts, she strode back to the car. She should get out of here while she could still determine where the road was.

To her disgust, "Rambo" Martin had fallen asleep in the cozy warmth inside the car.

I've got plenty to do, she thought as her car ground its way out of the drive. Best to put the Lords on the back shelf for a while.

Randall was sitting at his desk staring out of the window. Spring was beginning to show itself through old snow. His head felt cold. Victoria had shaved his head again last night and the heads of his little brothers. Her own hair she washed with a special soap and water she carried from the well and heated on the stove. Ms. Birchwood called his name. "Randall. Randall Lord."

Randall was yanked from his dreaming as if she had actually grabbed hold of his ear.

"Here," he answered automatically. The class howled with laughter.

"I *know* you're here," said Ms. Birchwood with exasperation. "I'm trying to find out if your mother or someone in your family will be coming on Parents' Day. That's the week after next."

Randall stared, confused. His father had been gone a long time—four, maybe five months. Gone, too, was the uneasy fear he always felt when Tom Lord was around. Randall hardly ever thought of him anymore. Sometimes he thought he saw the tracks of his father's old car in the driveway and a rush of fear prickled his skin. When he realized his uncle's motorcycle had made the tracks or some car had just turned around in their drive, his relief was so sharp it almost hurt him. Occasionally, when he passed by the gray side of the rotting barn, he remembered facing it for his beatings. "Out to the barn, boy," was his father's only instruction.

Parents' Day. His mother wouldn't come. She never left the house. Like a pale, unkempt ghost, she inhabited the shadowy rooms beneath the crumbling roof. Randall hated to go near her. She was so thin and wasted looking. She had toothaches all the time. Her face was usually crumpled with suffering. Being around his mother made Randall feel guilty and sorrowful. He always felt as if there were something he should do but he didn't know what it was. He grabbed his meals whenever his mother wasn't in the kitchen—bread and molasses, cold potatoes and canned peas.

"Randall?"

Randall was pulled back again into the class-room. Ms. Birchwood was standing with her hands on her narrow hips.

"Well?" she asked. "Will anyone from home be coming?"

Randall knew she expected him to say, "No." A stubborn knot tightened inside him.

"Luke," muttered Randall.

"I can't understand you, Randall, when you mumble," said Ms. Birchwood.

"My Uncle Luke," said Randall loudly.

Some kids snickered and he sent them a bewildered glare. Ms. Birchwood marked down something. "Last name?"

Randall squirmed.

"Does your uncle have a last name?"

Randall didn't know Uncle Luke's last name. Luke was his mother's brother. He came by often with groceries strapped onto his motorcycle. He never came when Randall's father was there and he never stayed long.

Randall curled down into his seat. Ms. Birchwood stared hard at him but then her expression softened.

"Okay, Randall. Good. I'm glad if your Uncle Luke can come."

Ms. Birchwood was grading papers. Randall Lord's spelling test had seventeen words out of twenty spelled right. His paper was smudgy and she was tempted to take off some points for untidiness. Sometimes his spelling papers were better than most of the others. Sometimes they were poor. Sometimes he didn't turn in a test. Though she couldn't include him among the talent and brains of her extraordinary fifth grade, she was finding it increasingly hard to act as though Randall Lord wasn't there.

He had drawn that beautiful picture of a deer in a wood. She wouldn't have believed that any fifth grader could draw that well if she hadn't seen him do it herself. And he had drawn other things. She had had glimpses of a big, black motorcycle, and marigolds, white with yellow shadows. Once she had seen him working on a pencil drawing of a window with rain on it—so real.

Randall always covered his drawings with his arm or slipped them into his big notebook before she got more than a brief look. There was something about his delicate, guarded manner that kept Ms. Birchwood from insisting on seeing what he had been drawing.

Besides, she really wanted as little as possible to do with Randall. He did his schoolwork in a decent enough handwriting marred only by smudges from his hands. She returned his papers and recorded his grades. She was marking time until she could pass him on to the sixth-grade teacher. She tried to ignore the things that caught her teacher's mind.

She stared at his paper. Randall Lord's name bothered her. Such an elegant name. *Lord.* Lord Randal. She searched her memory. There was an old poem, a Scottish ballad. Something about a Lord Randal—"*O where have you been, my handsome young man?*" She couldn't remember much of it except that it was sorrowful, the spelling was archaic, and Lord Randal was dying. *". . . Mother, mak my bed soon; I fain would lie doun."*

"Why am I dwelling on that child?" she asked herself impatiently. She wiped Randall from her mind and returned her thoughts to grading papers.

Randall was listening. The day was warm enough

for the windows to be open, and Randall was listening to spring sounds outside—water trickling somewhere, birds' flirting calls. Suddenly there was a hushed stir in the fifth-grade classroom and Randall looked up.

Everyone had stopped working to stare at a girl up in front of the room. Randall knew who she was. She had hair thick and dark as thunder, straight as rain. Her eyes were large and round, a dark hazel color. She was one of the smart kids in class and sort of crazy, too. She liked to wear weird clothes and lots of rings.

Today she was wearing a bullet belt filled with empty cartridges over a huge red T-shirt. One of her socks was red, the other yellow. She was also wearing a black eye. Her name was Jean Worth Neary.

The black eye fascinated Randall. He stopped daydreaming. All day he sneaked secret glances at the fascinating Jean. She sat at the front of the last row near the pencil sharpener.

Randall got up several times to sharpen his pencil. Her face, when he shot her a glance as he sharpened away, was sorrowful, her eyes big and glossy.

"Singapore," thought Randall. Outside of his

dreams, he had never seen anyone so beautiful.

Jean Worth Neary was not her usual self. She was full of indecision. She was furious with Edmond and Georgie for ganging up on her at the school bus stop that morning. Her fists weren't big enough and her size wasn't huge enough to punish them both properly. She would have liked to tell her father and bring down his wrath on them. But she didn't want her father to get all excited and mad and call up Edmond and Georgie's dad. Or worse, go to their house in a rage. Or come to school and visit the principal. She didn't want Edmond or Georgie calling her a wimp the next day for telling on them. She also didn't want to hear her mother remind her that she had to stick up for herself. "I *know* that," she muttered aloud.

Should she lie about the black eye when she got home? "I fell off the bus." Or, "I walked into an elbow." Or, "I don't know who threw the hot dog in my eye at lunch."

If she didn't tell her father, then she would have to confront Edmond and Georgie at the bus stop next morning. She'd been beating Georgie up since she was six. He used to call her "big mouth." Now he called her "Charles Bronson" and then ran away. He was a sniveling little beast. But his brother Edmond was three years older and BIG! Heavy, too. Edmond never actually touched her, but he was *there*, egging little Georgie on.

I'll tell Dad I ran into the teeter-totter, she decided. I'll walk to the next bus stop in the morning. "I'll have to get up fifteen minutes earlier—I think—about," she muttered. "Dad will be buried in his newspaper or at the typewriter or out in the garden. I may have to explain to Mom why I'm leaving so early, but her eyes will be half closed and her mind will be at work already."

Jean was disappointed when she got home that nobody paid much attention to her black eye. Her mother examined it only long enough to see if the eye was all right. Moriah, her teenage sister, said she looked like a Cabbage Patch criminal. Her dad joked, "I'd hate to see the other guy." That was all the sensation she caused.

The next morning she forgot to get up early. She told herself to hurry, but instead she poked through washing and brushing and breakfast, as usual. Then she hoped that Moriah would take the bus partway with her instead of driving to the high school with her boyfriend in his crippled car. But

25

Moriah's boyfriend showed up, clattering to a halt in their gravel driveway. Alone, Jean dragged her feet to the bus stop, hoping to arrive at the same time as the bus.

The bus was nowhere in sight. When she got close, she saw Georgie and Edmond were there, slapping at each other in a disinterested fashion. She halted by a bush, hoping someone else would show up. To her surprise, she saw Randall Lord trudging up to her bus stop. He usually got on the bus earlier, farther up the road. Big Edmond spied Jean and whispered something to Georgie, giving him a nudge.

"Hey, wimp, tell your da-dee?" mocked Edmond.

"Hey, wimp, like your black eye?" yelled little Georgie shrilly.

Jean felt her blood begin to boil. Fear and anger sent hot tears into her eyes. Her head felt light. She clenched her fists into knots and marched blindly toward Georgie. He stopped, whined, and tried to slide behind Edmond. Edmond pushed him out in front and yelled, "Go get the little wimp, Georgie!"

Jean stabbed her fists into the air in front of her, practicing. Georgie wrestled against Edmond, who yelled, "Kill, kill, Georgie boy!"

Suddenly Randall Lord was there. He stood in front of Georgie. Georgie crumpled against his big brother. Edmond's mouth opened. "Get outta here, Lord," he said, but he backed off, too.

"Leave her alone," said Randall Lord. The two boys backed away together as Randall advanced toward them.

The bus arrived. The brothers hurriedly stumbled on. Jean jumped into the bus behind Randall, who headed toward the back, where his sister Victoria sat alone on the wide last seat.

Jean hesitated, then, still standing, she called, "Hey, Randall." He turned his head. "Talk to you at recess," she said. She glared at her astounded classmates, at her friends. "Randall just saved Georgie's life," she announced and flopped into a seat next to Paul Lunde.

Randall was in a glow. He couldn't wait until recess. Usually he stood by the swings waiting to grab one. When he finally got a swing, everyone else went someplace else. Randall was not surprised. It was part of his wall. He was so used to his wall he'd forgotten it. Without understanding why, he expected people to avoid him. Most of his school life had worked this way.

But today he would talk with Jean Worth Neary at recess. He would get to examine her black eye up close. Maybe he would reach through the wall and touch her sleeve.

On the noisy playground Jean seemed to have forgotten her promise. She was jumping rope, Double Dutch, with three other girls. They had dumped their coats in a pile on the ground. Randall slumped into a dream of motorcycles.

He was startled out of his dream by her voice.

"Thanks, Randall," said Jean. "You kept me from killing Georgie."

Randall stood speechless with surprise and delight. He was afraid to look into her eyes, so he stared at Jean's chin, concentrating on a tiny scar in the middle. He couldn't think of a single thing to say to keep her there.

"Well," said Jean, turning to go, "just thought I'd tell you."

"Who gave you the black eye?" blurted Randall in a rush.

Jean halted. He dared to look at the skin around her black eye. It was purple with a mustard yellow smear through the center.

"Georgie did it," said Jean angrily. "I've been

28

beating him up since I was six years old. But he's hard to take on with sludgebrain Edmond around."

"Edmond's afraid of me," said Randall eagerly—holding Jean there.

"You've got to be deranged," she said. "They're not *afraid* of you—at least Edmond isn't."

"They backed off," argued Randall. Jean looked at him in surprise.

"Everybody backs off from you," she said, "or haven't you noticed?"

Jean, herself, while she spoke to him, was standing off and leaning away. He looked again at her face, at the large dark eyes, at the purple-yellow bruise. Then he dropped his head. Right then, he didn't want the wall there.

"How do you get them to play?" he mumbled. Then, louder, he asked, "How do you get them to stay on the swings? How do you get them to give you a black eye?"

Jean stared at him. Then she asked casually, like asking for the time, "When was the last time you had a bath?"

"A bath? You mean in a tub—with water?"

"No, with Kool-Aid," said Jean.

Randall looked so startled and serious that

Jean added, "Just kidding, Randall."

Randall explored her face, looking for clues, answers to his questions.

"You just need . . ." Jean paused. "You need to try and snaz up a little," she said. "Maybe a bath or two. I mean, water's free."

"We don't have any water," Randall told her.

"Get real. Everybody has water," said Jean. "Try looking in the bathroom."

Randall turned away in despair. "It doesn't work," he mumbled.

"What!" Jean hollered after him. "What doesn't work? Where do you go to the bathroom?"

Randall thought of the outhouse behind his home, back by an old garden filled with weeds and volunteer squash. His father used to sit there with his gun and shoot at the rabbits that had come to nibble.

"Randall! Yo-oh! Randall!" Jean called him back. "What're you thinking? Where'd you go?"

Randall turned back to Jean, facing her. "We have an outhouse in back. But I go to the school bathroom," he told her, "like everybody else."

"Wow," said Jean softly. "Wow. An outhouse. I didn't think anyone had that kind of thing in real life. Just in the comics or at Eagle Lake." Her hazel eyes got even darker. "That's a real problem."

When the end-of-recess bell rang, Jean walked, head bent in thought, back to the classroom. She barely noticed her friend Kendra, who ran to catch up.

Randall was dreaming of water. Sitting at his desk, he dreamed of streams and waterfalls. He dreamed of showers from the sky washing everything clean. He dreamed of thunderstorms with lightning. The rain was crashing to earth; lightning struck his house, driving dirt from corners. It electrified his bed, driving hidden insects from the gray sheets.

The rain fell and fell, washing sheets and towels, washing Victoria and his little brothers, easing his mother's terrible toothaches.

Jean Worth Neary was smiling at him through a rainy window.

Jean wasn't sure she liked Randall Lord. She was so used to being turned off by him, by the dirt and the smell and the threat of lice. Besides, nobody else liked him. She didn't have a carload of friends herself—one really good girlfriend, Kendra. They

31

played "crash diet" together, imagining their bodies getting slimmer and slimmer. They played "pick up dudes," swaying by imaginary video game houses. Then they played "eating binge," devouring frozen slush on a stick and cold hot dogs dipped in mayonnaise. Some of the kids in her class liked Jean because of her cheerful boldness and because she always had something unexpected and outrageous to say. But a carload of friends? Nah.

Randall Lord was another story. She kept remembering how he had walked toward Edmond and Georgie. "Leave her alone," he had said. She kept remembering the intense look he had flashed her on the bus out of his violet-blue eyes.

"He could be a friend if he cleans up his act," said Jean to herself—and added, "A week in a bathtub might do the trick."

Randall was worrying. He hadn't seen Uncle Luke to ask him to visit school on Parents' Day. He had missed Luke two nights ago when he came by to bring Randall's mother some flat yellow pills for her toothaches. Now her face was relaxed, her arms graceful and slow. She moved through the house as if she was underwater. Yesterday she had tried to do some washing but it had taken her all day, bringing in water from the rusty pump, slowly sloshing the clothes and towels up and down in the tub. Randall had helped carry water and soap the clothes. After his mother had rinsed them, Randall had helped spread them on bushes to dry.

But when his mother had gone to pull the sheets from the beds, she had given a little cry. Randall had seen, for the first time, little bugs scuttling for cover under the mattress. His mother had left the sheets there crumpled across the bed.

Last night they had slept outdoors on the clean towels spread across the grass. It had gotten cold before morning and they had all wound up cuddled together in a nest of towels.

Randall didn't know when his Uncle Luke would come by again. Maybe he could write him a letter. Maybe his mother could give him Luke's address. And Luke's last name. Maybe Victoria knew. Parents' Day was next week. He would have to write the letter right away.

Jean read the letter before Randall mailed it. "I'll be your editor," she said.

They were the only ones sitting on the swings at

recess. Randall wore a somewhat clean shirt. Jean read the letter out loud.

> *Dear Uncle Luke,*
>   *Will you come to Parents' Day next Thursday? Ma will be home sleeping from the pills or sick from the toothaches and can't come. All the parents come and talk to the teacher. They would let an uncle come. You could talk to Victoria's teacher, too, but not Toby's or Jacob's teacher since they don't have real schoolwork yet.*
>   *Thank you very much.*
>   *Your nephew,*
>   *Randall*

"I think you should use 'please'," said Jean. She also suggested Randall ask after his uncle's health at the beginning of the letter. Jean used a red pencil to make suggestions in the margins. She added the date after Thursday. She added: *I really miss you.* Then she added, *P.S. You could give me and my friend, Jean, a ride on your motorcycle at that time and kill two birds with one stone.*

While Randall and Jean were working on the letter, some other kids gathered near the swings out of curiosity to listen to Jean as she read the revised version of Randall's letter. Paul Lunde offered a comment, "That sounds good, Randall. I hope your uncle comes. I'd like a look at that motorcycle."

Randall looked up, surprised, and smiled.

The next day Jean brought him an envelope with a stamp on it. An art museum's name and address were crossed off in the left corner. Randall had gotten his uncle's last name and address from an old birthday card sent to his mother. He wrote it neatly across the front. Jean gave the envelope to Ms. Birchwood and asked that it go out with the school mail that day. "Randall's uncle needs to get this right away," she explained. Ms. Birchwood looked surprised and then a little annoyed, but Jean was hard to resist when she was being earnest. Ms. Birchwood shook her head but she said, "Take it to Miss Wyeth at the office."

Randall was drawing. He drew two large, glossy eyes like a deer's eyes. Then he drew Jean Worth Neary's face around the eyes with a pencil. He colored in a purple-and-mustard yellow bruise around one eye. Jean's real black eye was almost gone now, and Randall wanted one to look at once in a while.

At recess, he smuggled the drawing outside. He

stood by the building, trying to locate Jean. Once he spied her he wasn't sure he wanted her to notice him, wasn't sure he wanted to show her his drawing. He wasn't certain but she might throw it in the wastebasket. He watched her jump in and out of whirring Double Dutch ropes turned by Tiffany and Kendra. Her forehead was clenched with concentration, her hair flew out like the wing of a dark bird. Randall slipped back into the classroom to do another drawing. He placed his first Jean drawing next to Singapore inside his notebook. Then he drew Jean jumping with her hair flying, two blurred ropes flying.

It was not easy to draw flying ropes, but Randall could draw difficult things.

Although school was no longer the treat it had been when he started in first grade, Randall didn't share the whoop and holler of relief most students gave at the end of the school day. Going home wasn't anything he looked forward to, even though he could drop his wall there.

Sometimes, on good weather days, Randall slipped off the school bus earlier than his stop so he could walk by Burger Barn. The warm, smoky odor of grilling hamburgers lay heavy in the air for blocks, and that made it worth Randall's while to walk the extra four miles home.

His Uncle Luke had stopped once at the Burger Barn takeout window while Randall sat on the throbbing motorcycle behind him. Burgers and fries had been handed out in a crackling clean bag. Randall never forgot the warmth of the bag he carried pressed against Luke's back as they rode home, or the hot meaty smell that rose richly into his face. He could call it all to mind any time he was hungry, which was a good share of each day. On the backs of returned English papers, on the backs of his spelling tests, he drew hamburgers— the thickness of meat juicily nesting in soft buns. He drew crisp fingers of french fries poking out of a cardboard triangle.

One day, as Randall stepped from the bus behind the regulars who got off at the Burger Barn stop, Jean jumped out noisily behind him. She waved a pass at the driver and the bus door closed.

"It's a year-old pass," she giggled at Randall and tucked the pass carefully in one of her coat pockets. "I use it all the time."

It had never occurred to Randall to try and obtain a pass. He stood in startled silence sorting out a confusion of feelings. His anticipation of enjoying the odor of hot food battled with his pleasure and discomfort at Jean's unexpected nearness.

"Going for a burger?" asked Jean.

"Uh—no," labored Randall, "I—uh—just like the smell."

"I have extra money," said Jean. "Want a burger?"

Randall's mind spun. Did he ever want one! Could he let Jean buy him one? What did she want from him? What was *extra* money? What would it be like *inside* Burger Barn? He felt his heart tighten. He held his breath while he steadied his defenses.

Jean, misreading his hesitation, said, "It's okay. They have a bathroom. You can wash your hands. And arms, for that matter." She stopped and looked seriously at him. "You could wash your face, too, if you wanted."

Juices began to seep unchecked in Randall's mouth.

"Come on," said Jean. "I don't want to go home yet. No one's there right now. It's too lonely."

That did it. His defenses routed, Randall walked into Burger Barn for the first time in his life. As soon as they pushed through the glass doors, Jean pointed out the bathrooms.

"I'm going to wash my hands, too," she announced. Randall wondered why but was grateful for any delay in this new adventure.

It was a clean, new-looking bathroom, empty now. There was hot water to run in the sink, soap, and plenty of paper towels. Randall washed his hands, and they changed color. His nails looked dirtier now. A wave of panic swept through him and he decided not to wash his arms. Then he decided to leave. He wasn't hungry anymore. No burger was worth being this uncomfortable.

But Jean knocked on the door. "Randall," she called in a loud stage whisper. "Come on. I've ordered burgers already. Hope you like cheese."

Randall would never dream of violating the privacy of the girls' bathroom by knocking on the door. His awe of Jean increased.

The light was soft and amber colored in the place where tables and booths were. The air was heavy with the smell and sizzle of food. Clear voices called out orders in a fascinating code. *"Double without. Deep-six the Coke."*

In one corner, some laughing high school kids had jammed themselves into a booth. A few mothers were there with small children. There were some old people, too, and a few students he recognized from school. He only had to shut out a few stares. It wasn't so bad.

Jean led him to a booth. Two square paper-wrapped bundles sat on a tray and two large Cokes with straws already stuck in them.

"Dinner is served, m' lord," she said elegantly and bowed low with a sweep of her arm. Then she giggled. "Whoops! M'Randall Lord, that is. I made an accidental pun."

Randall smiled and sat down in the amber light. He unwrapped the fragrant bundle. In no time, his cheeseburger was gone, chewed and swallowed. He smelled the paper, then folded it neatly and put it in his pocket.

He couldn't believe how slowly Jean ate. She talked a lot and chewed carefully, swallowing before she spoke again. She sucked up Coke. Randall would not remember, later, much of anything she said. It was something about being the only kid in a family with three "brilliant" adults. Apparently she had a "brilliant" mother and a "brilliant" father and a "brilliant" sister and it was all some kind of hardship. But Randall barely listened. This adventure had begun to have a dangerous feel to it. He was eager to leave yet mesmerized by Jean's lips shaping words and then taking in small bites of food. He couldn't keep his eyes off the remainder of her hamburger as she pushed it away.

"Let's go," she said. "I've got this really *great* idea!"

As they slid from their seats, Randall snatched the rest of her hamburger and stuffed it into his pants pocket.

"We have this enormous bathroom—big enough for a stage production of *The Wizard of Oz*." Jean Worth Neary's big eyes got bigger when she exaggerated. "With a complete cast of Munchkins." They were crunching up the gravel drive to the Neary house, Randall behind Jean. Randall was hunched up and kept his eyes fastened on the bullet belt Jean wore over a purple T-shirt today. She was carrying her coat. Randall had stopped wearing his winter jacket as soon as the weather had warmed. It had been donated by the Ladies of Charity, and Mike Spellman at school had recognized it as his big brother's cast-off clothing. "The cat puked on it once," he told Randall with a snigger. Randall hated the jacket.

Now he stepped carefully as though he and Jean were making their way through a minefield.

Jean was pretty certain no one was home. Her dad was at a PTO meeting at school. He was the president and the only man who came to the PTO

41

meetings. This both embarrassed and pleased Jean. Her mom was the director of a fine arts museum in the city and would almost surely be at "some big meeting or other," Jean told Randall. "This'll be quite private, I assure you."

In the doorway of the big, handsome old house she called, "Hello? Anyone home?" No one answered.

"Come on in," said Jean, "but don't touch anything. The best bathroom's off my mom and dad's room. They sleep downstairs."

The Neary best bathroom turned out to be as big as the living room at Randall's run-down house. It had a clean white tile floor and a huge, spanking clean tub in pale yellow. Everything was yellow— the big, thick towels, the toilet and sink. Yellow curtains billowed at the window. Randall stood in the doorway looking lost.

But Jean had no time for a lost boy. Someone could come home at any moment and find her with this filthy kid. She couldn't even count on Moriah's silence without some kind of bribe. Moriah would probably want to trade bedrooms.

Jean started the water in the tub and poured in a long, thick stream of bubble bath. A lovely smell began to fill the room.

"Okay, into the tub," commanded Jean.

Randall balked, panic in his face. "I won't take a bath with you in the room."

"You're not going to take off your clothes," argued Jean. "Just get in. Even your tennis shoes need to be washed. You can't put on those dirty duds over a pure-clean bod."

Randall stared. He hadn't thought about his clothes, about what to put on after he took this bath.

"You can scrub your clothes while you're scrubbing yourself," explained Jean. She had thought this out at Burger Barn. "I just want to make sure you're clean. Maybe I should go get some bleach. That kills germs, you know."

"What do I do then?" protested Randall in a strangled voice. He was getting more upset. "Stand in the sun till I dry?"

"That's a pretty funny idea," said Jean. She hoo-hooed a throaty giggle. Then she cocked her head in thought. "Well, I bet Moriah's jeans will fit you, and one of my T-shirts."

"Girl's clothes?" Randall was made bold by outrage. "I don't wear girls' clothes."

"I don't wear girls' clothes either," said Jean, hoo-hooing again. "My T-shirt is really my dad's, and Moriah only wears boys' jeans. Only Calvin Kleins."

43

"I can't," said Randall, backing away. His voice fell to a whisper. "I said I would, but I can't do it."

"Sure you can," cried Jean in frustration. "Look, it's easy." Without another thought, without removing her tennis shoes or her rings or her notorious bullet belt, Jean stepped smartly into the tub of foaming water.

The foam rose slightly, and Jean leaned and turned off the faucet. Then she sat down. The water came dangerously close to the top of the tub.

"See," she said, laughing now. "It's fun." She picked up the soap and began vigorously to scrub her arms.

"Okay, now your turn," she said, standing up. The water ran from her clothing like a hundred open faucets. Her shirt was stuck to her and her new jeans looked leaden. "I bet I weigh a ton," she said, "with all this water in my clothes." She stepped dripping from the tub and sloshed to the corner where she stood on a scale. "Yeeps!" she exclaimed. "Look how much I weigh!"

Randall had been standing shocked but now he began to smile in disbelief.

"Come on, Randall," cried Jean. "Let's conduct an experiment."

Randall's smile widened expectantly.

"We'll weigh you now, *sans* water. *Sans*—that

means without . . . We'll weigh you without water. Then you get into the tub. Then, after, we'll weigh you wet."

It took no coaxing to get Randall onto the scales. It took no coaxing to get Randall into the tub. The water turned first a coffee-with-cream color and then deepened, when he sat down, to chocolate. The suds sat on top, popping softly and dying.

Randall stood up, eager to be weighed, but Jean pushed him back down into the water, gingerly using one finger.

"Scrub, Randall, scrub first," she said. And Randall began to scrub. The soap was fat and yellow and smelled like lemons. He soaped his arms and legs, his T-shirt and pants. The remainder of Jean's burger suddenly floated to the surface. Randall sank it in a hurry before Jean could notice. Then he scrubbed at his tennis shoes. The water grew darker. He soaped the back of his neck and the soft pale bristles of hair that were growing back on his head.

Jean removed her tennis shoes and went, dribbling water, to her room and then to her sister's to fetch clothing for the two of them. Randall was standing, dripping and shivering, when she returned. Both of them had forgotten about weighing Randall wet. Jean was in a hurry now to get the dressing over with before anyone came home. Randall sensed her growing anxiety. He, too, was in a hurry to get out of there.

"Use a yellow towel," yelled Jean. She grabbed one for herself and threw clothes for Randall onto a chair. "I'll dress in my room. Hurry up!" She closed the bathroom door, leaving Randall worrying about which yellow towel to use.

It was then that they both heard the automobile drive round to the back of the house. A car door slammed. The back door slammed.

"Jean!" called Jean's mother. "Moriah? Someone! Come help me unload the groceries."

Randall was thinking. He had stripped off his wet clothes and shoes. He had dried himself on a thick yellow towel. The strange woman's voice still pounded in his ears. Randall was thinking—fast thinking whirling amid flashes of fear inside his head. He was yanking on unfamiliar jeans and thinking. Should he jump out of the window, wet clothes under his arms? He didn't want to abandon Jean, though. Would she be in more trouble if he left? Or if he stayed?

The bathroom floor was covered with gray water. Water was struggling down the drain with a sucking chug. The tub was black with dirt, a greasy darker ring encircling the inside like a filthy belt. Randall remembered the sunken burger and searched frantically through the muddy water until he found the soggy ruins. He flushed it down the toilet.

The door opened a crack and Jean's arm tossed in a dirty yellow towel and her soggy clothes. "Hurry up and meet my mother," she hissed through the crack.

When Jean's mother came back in on her second trip from the car, arms loaded with groceries, she was met by her daughter, *sans* bullet belt and wearing her T-shirt backward. The ends of her hair were wet. Standing nervously behind her daughter was a handsome boy with deep blue eyes and a shaved head, wearing an identical shirt, also on backward. "New style," thought Mrs. Neary. She also noticed that the boy wore Calvin Klein jeans that came way down over bare feet.

"His family's rich," thought Jean's mother, "or else he's coerced them into buying Calvin's the way Moriah does us."

For a reason she would have despised if she'd recognized it in herself, Mrs. Neary felt comforted by the expensive jeans. Randall looked like the sons of lots of people she knew and dealt with. While the youngsters were bringing the rest of the groceries in, she wearily took off her shoes.

"I'll feel better after a hot bath," she muttered aloud to no one in particular.

"What would your dad have done, given you a whippin'?" asked Randall, hoisting a sack of potatoes out of the car, ". . . if he'd caught us?"

"A what?" asked Jean, "a whipping? We don't do that. We have to have this talk—this long, l-o-o-ng talk—this discussion. Whipping would be easier—and over faster. They keep asking, 'Do you understand?' and even if you say, 'Yes,' they go over it all again. Then you have to give your opinion, which means you have to think about it some more. Give me a whipping any day."

Randall eyed her in disbelief. Maybe she'd never been whipped. He watched her elbow the back door open, arms around a great bag of groceries. It was then that the terrible scream came from the bathroom. They both stopped in their tracks.

Randall was remembering. He thought about Jean's mother, who screamed when she was excited. He shivered, remembering the soft touch of her fingers on his back as she ushered him back to the bathroom with one hand, Jean with the other. The bathroom had resembled a battleground.

"What were you *doing* in here? Washing a tree?" Jean's mother had asked. Her voice was full and stern. Her eyes swept the room, taking in the grimy tub, the black fingermarks on the yellow soap, the devastated towels. Two pairs of soggy tennis shoes were sitting in their own gray puddles.

Randall was awed by Jean's calm answer. "Well, you see, Randall needed a bath . . ."

"I guess so!" exclaimed Jean's mother.

"I didn't need one much but I had to convince Randall—and his clothes needed a bath, too, and his tennis shoes. . . ."

"I'm hearing you, Jean," said her mother, "but I'm not getting anything."

Randall was remembering how Jean's mother waited for Jean to explain.

"Why did you both take a bath? You didn't take one together, did you?"

"*No*," exploded Jean. "You think I'm crazy? We

kept our clothes on anyway. I took one first to encourage Randall. You see, he's a little shy—but he was desperate to take a bath."

"Jean," her mother had said, "we're going to have to have a good, long talk."

Randall remembered Jean's groan and how she rolled her eyes I-told-you-so at him. No wonder Jean could work miracles. She had a magic family with a powerful queen for a mother.

"I can't believe anyone could have been that dirty!" Jean's mother was talking to Jean's father that night, after the grand bathroom affair.

"Jean gave him *my* jeans—my *Calvins!*" raged Moriah for the fifteenth time. "I think she would have let him wear them home. To Bedbug Heaven."

The family was sitting in the kitchen at their round oak table, except for Jean's dad, who was peeling onions by the sink. He held a piece of bread in his mouth, which he said kept him from crying over the onion. Jean's mother was sipping a glass of pinkish wine.

"I almost saved the bathroom the way it *was* to show you," continued Jean's mother. "But I was desperate for a bath." Here she eyed Jean. "Maybe as desperate as your Randall."

Jean had been drooping in her chair. But her head flew up and she said defiantly, "He *was* desperate. Nobody likes him. He has literally no friends." She looked at her mother directly. "*You* wanted a luxury bath. Randall needed a bath to get clean. It's like if you wanted cherries jubilee after dinner but Randall just wants dinner."

Jean's father took the bread from his mouth. "That's enough, Jean," he said in his stop-it-right-now voice.

"I wanted a *medicinal* bath," corrected Jean's mother, "to revive me after slaving all day for this family."

"That's enough, my macho wife," said Jean's father in the same tone of voice. He put the bread back in his mouth like a period stopping the words in a sentence.

"Jean would bring home every lost kitten in the world," said Moriah, "if you let her." She was lounging with one arm dangling carelessly on the back of the chair. Moriah always lounged, even when she ran the vacuum cleaner. "Every lost dog . . . every lost gerbil . . . every lost fish . . ."

Jean's mother took a sip of her wine. "So did I,"

she murmured, her face softening, "when I was her age."

Jean's father paused and then said, muffled through the bread, "So did I."

"Randall's not a lost kitten," insisted Jean.

"Randall Lord," mused Jean's mother. "Strange name. 'Lord Randal, my son . . .' "

" 'O where hae ye been, Lord Randal, my son?' " quoted Jean's father, the bread now swallowed. He began to slice yellow peppers.

" 'O where hae ye been, my handsome young man?' " remembered Jean's mother, her voice lyrical and sweet.

" 'I hae been to the greenwood; mother mak my bed soon,' " answered Jean's father, " 'for I'm wearied wi' hunting and fain wad lie doun.' " He turned to smile at his wife.

" 'Wild wood,' not 'greenwood,' " corrected Jean's mother.

"There are many versions," explained Jean's father. "And many different spellings. No one knows who wrote the poem. Before Shakespeare's time. The English claim it. So do the Scots. I once found a version in a book called *American Folk Poetry*."

"Randall *is* handsome," said Jean, joining her

parents' dreamy discussion. "And he's nice and he's helpful."

Her father was about to drop the chopped and sliced vegetables into the wok, but he stopped. He put down the bowl of onions and peppers and broccoli and turned to Jean.

"You may have coerced Randall into bathing this once, Jean," he said seriously, "but he goes home to sleep in his clothes. He goes home to dirty sheets and probably bedbugs."

"I noticed bites on his arms," said Jean's mother, the soft voice gone.

"What bites!" cried Jean angrily. "I didn't see any bites." But she had seen them. She'd noticed them clearly after the filth was rubbed away, leaving Randall with white-white, blond-haired arms, dotted here and there with little red marks. "I think that was freckles," she said stubbornly.

"The point is, Jean," said her father, "he has no way to keep it up. In a week he'll be nearly as dirty as before today."

"It's not his fault," cried Jean. Tears of sorrow and frustration flooded her eyes. "He really wants to be clean. He's a good person. He sticks up for me. I like him. He's almost my friend." Jean wasn't too distraught to notice her parents' hesitation.

"Who else has he got?" she wailed. Then, calmly, she played her trump card, reminding her father of one of his constant sayings. "Aren't we supposed to be responsible for our fellow man?"

Jean's mother and father looked at each other helplessly. Moriah sighed and shifted her position languidly. "Looks like we've got another cat," she said.

Randall was smiling to himself. He remembered the feel of the pile of wet yellow towels and clothing he carried to the Neary laundry room. There he and Jean had stuffed them into the washing machine except for Jean's purple shirt. "Bleach'll kill this shirt and I love the color. Don't you love the color?" Randall loved the color.

Jean poured detergent into the machine and pushed some buttons. Water began to fill the washer. Then they lugged the mop to the bathroom. First they rinsed the tub with hot water and scoured it, rinsed it again.

"And I was embarrassed about *my* tub rings," hooted Jean. Then they mopped the floor. Randall used a mop for the first time in his life. They had to put the bathroom scale outdoors in the sun to dry.

Randall relived the afternoon over and over in his mind. He could recall each detail as clear as well water. Mrs. Neary inspected the bathroom, shaking her head as she put out clean yellow towels. But she said, "Good job, you guys." Randall remembered her voice, which had many notes in it. He remembered the way she stood. He remembered her hair which was thick and curly as field bushes. The afternoon had been as much fun as Uncle Luke's motorcycle.

At home, Victoria said, "What happened to you?" Randall was wearing his own clothes, many shades cleaner. Then Victoria asked, "What are those? Bites on your arms?"

The spring night was warm and Randall decided to sleep outdoors on towels again. They weren't as clean as last week. He had a curious, lightheaded feeling. Victoria brought towels, too, and stretched out nearby. His little brothers curled together like puppies under some old coats on the tumbled porch. Their mother sat there, an exhausted shadow, in an old rocker.

Randall's dreams started out pleasant enough. Uncle Luke came sailing out of the sky on his motorcycle, which Randall could direct with remote control. Then Uncle Luke became invisible—

only his motorcycle kept going around and around in the school parking lot.

Randall woke up in the morning worried about Uncle Luke and wondering if he had gotten his letter.

Luke Meriweather worried about his sister, Veery, all the time. Leaning into the engine of a car he was repairing, her suffering face would slip into his mind. He was a good mechanic. He tried not to let his worries interfere with his job at the Honda garage. But, hoisting the body of a four-door on the big lift, he pictured Veery's scabby, run-wild children. Staring into the dark, oily innards of a chuckling motor, he was haunted by the memory of the empty cupboards at the Lord home. And he hated Tom Lord.

Veery was two years older than Luke, but he felt like she was his baby sister. He remembered her as a shy, smiling girl who liked to draw flowers and then as a blushing teenager with long, pale hair. She had taught him to catch a ball and, later, to dance. When she was seventeen, hopeful and quiet, she had married handsome Tom Lord. He was thirty-two. It wasn't long before the shy hopefulness wore out. Her quietness deepened. The shine disappeared from Veery's eyes.

Some misery just happens, thought Luke. Veery's bad teeth and her three miscarriages after Butterfly was born—those were probably just bad luck. But the misery Tom Lord inflicted on his family wasn't necessary or natural.

Luke knew that when Tom Lord was home, he was either angry or drunk. He knew that Tom Lord beat Veery. Luke guessed that Lord beat the kids, too, whenever he happened to notice them. But Veery's kids were good at staying out of their father's way.

Sometimes, whenever Tom Lord was gone, Luke gave the kids rides on his motorcycle. The oldest boy, Randall, seemed sort of wild, so Luke took the kid hunting with him once. Just to get him off Veery's hands for a bit, give the kid something real to do. But Randall went white as a picket fence over Luke's first kill and then moped worse than Veery.

"Never again," Luke told himself. "These aren't my problems. Nothing I can do." But Veery's lost face followed him around. The one time Luke tried to directly interfere with Tom Lord was after he'd found Veery on the floor with a swollen face and welts all over her arms. Luke had grabbed Tom Lord out of his car where he sat with a bottle in a paper bag. He slammed the half-drunk man against the hood.

"My God, man, what's wrong with you?" he'd roared into his face. "You leave her be, Tom. Take your garbage out on someone your size. But leave Veery alone!"

Tom Lord didn't try to fight Luke. Luke, though not a fighting man, was lean and tough. But that night, Tom Lord set fire to Luke's new motorcycle. Next day, Lord made threatening telephone calls to Luke's boss at the Honda garage. Luke lost a motorcycle and almost lost his job. The Honda service manager didn't want to let a top mechanic like Luke go, but he didn't want any trouble either.

Luke took to sneaking groceries to Veery till he could figure out what better to do. He brought her pills to ease her toothaches. One time he looked into dental insurance at work, but he'd have to be the head of the household for Veery to get any benefits. And he'd have to be around to talk Veery out of the house and into a dentist's office. "When am I gonna get on with my own life?" he sometimes wondered aloud.

Luke's attempts to save money for some half-imagined future were defeated by what he spent on his sister behind Tom Lord's back. Welfare money for the Lord family was out of the question. Tom Lord would be enraged if the government stuck its nose into his business. Besides, Luke was sure Veery wasn't up to the song and dance she'd have to perform for welfare checks.

In the eight years he'd worked as a mechanic, Luke had only managed to save about $460, barely enough to get on with his life. And he didn't see how he could do much more for his sister, never knowing when Tom Lord might show up. The man was crazy, and Luke didn't want to bring down more grief on Veery than she already had.

"It's a no-win situation," Luke told himself. His helplessness frustrated him. It was his sister he was thinking of, not her kids. He couldn't get past Veery's silent suffering to see that her handsome children were being twisted out of shape. Except for Butterfly, who'd flown away.

Then, one day, he received a letter from Randall. Luke never got real letters, just bills and junk mail. In surprise, Luke opened his letter.

Randall missed him. Randall wanted to know how he was. Randall wanted him to come to school on Parents' Day and talk to his teacher.

Randall had a friend to impress with his Uncle Luke's motorcycle.

Luke felt the weight of his sister grow heavier. Now Randall had become someone real, not just Veery's baggage or a tag-along on a deer hunt.

"What'm I gonna do?" said Luke to himself. "Run away like Tom? Sometime I gotta start my own life."

After reading the letter again, Luke felt a tremendous urge to escape to the movies. He wanted to laugh or sweat or cry over something that wasn't real. Instead he went to a bar where he knew Tom Lord used to hang out.

Ms. Birchwood didn't look inside her students' desks. It was a principle with her. Their desks were their domain, she felt—their private space.

But she knew instinctively that Tiffany Spizinski's desk was neat and orderly inside. Tiffany could lay her hands on anything she needed with just one look.

Ms. Birchwood knew without looking that the contents of Paul Lunde's desk were squared off and that Lynda Percherman probably had everything shoved to one side so she could pick at cupcakes hidden in front. Kendra Crosswhite kept every school paper she ever got back with an A. Ms. Birchwood supposed, since Kendra got A's on everything, that her desk was stuffed with old tests and compositions. Mike Spellman kept a library book open to steal glances at whenever he lifted his desk top. She suspected that Jean Worth Neary's desk was a clutter of school things and found things and favorite things, like magic trick cards and bounce-high balls, even though Jean could reach her hand inside without looking and find what she wanted.

But Ms. Birchwood had only a few hints as to what was inside Randall Lord's desk. She often paused by it at recess time or after school, tempted. In her mind's eye she saw that big, dog-eared notebook Randall always eased in and out of his desk. Where inside that notebook, she wondered, was the deer with the red heart?

It was after school on Tuesday, two days before Parents' Day, that Ms. Birchwood gave in to temptation. She had stayed late, giving her room final touches for the big event. The science project and the Indian village her students had finished were set up. She had tacked up the "If I Won the Lottery" essays, the limericks, and the blank verse.

Now she was leafing through student artwork, deciding which drawings to pin to the freshly covered display board and which to put outside in the hall. Some of her students were good artists but a feeling of dissatisfaction dogged her. She couldn't choose.

Then the deer with the red heart surfaced to the top of her mind. Without another thought, she got up and marched straight to Randall Lord's desk and flipped up the top.

It was a neat, rather barren interior. How was it she hadn't known? The big notebook sat in the center. An old flat tin box held worn crayons arranged by color and shade. Another box held four stubby pencils and a pen that said "A-1 Cycle Shop." There were no erasers on the pencils. Five felt-tip markers were next to the pencil box.

Reverently Ms. Birchwood picked up the notebook. The name B U T T E R F L Y L. printed on the worn cloth cover had almost faded out. It was a ring binder, but most of the pages were school paper with no holes. All of the paper was lined. All of the paper carried drawings. On the backs of returned spelling tests and grammar studies were drawings in pencil and crayon, drawings in ink. There were drawings of desks and daisies, of students and students' hands, of hamburgers and fries. There was a pen sketch of Tiffany Spizinski's patent leather tap shoes and her ankles with lace-edged socks. She lifted a page that had a pencil sketch of Paul Lunde's profile with his happy smirk. Ms. Birchwood found the black motorcycle, and Jean Neary's face filling an entire page.

"Oh," Ms. Birchwood kept breathing out as she lifted each one. "My goodness!"

She gasped in pleased surprise when she discovered a page devoted to her—her profile at the chalkboard, her hands on her hips over her favorite pleated skirt, and herself sitting at her desk, fingers at her brow.

Then she came across an unbelievable drawing of Jean Neary jumping between two blurred lines of rope.

Slowly she sat down in Randall's seat and began to look through the drawings again. She sat there for a long time until her knees began to stiffen.

Randall was waiting. Usually he waited by the left door of the big entrance to the school for the bell to ring. The other students gathered by the right door in a crowded huddle.

Randall always waited facing the fields or the

playground, his eyes distant and dreaming. But today Randall faced the door with his head down. He had this awful feeling as if a light was shining on him, illuminating the red bites on his arms. His clothes didn't feel as stiff as when they were first washed but they were so clean. He could still smell the soap in them. He didn't feel real.

Jean Worth Neary had not gotten on the bus today. Victoria had been no help when the strangeness had seeped into him through his clean clothes as he made his way to the back seat. All during the ride to school he had felt a dread mounting in him.

Now, on the steps behind him, there was some hushed whispering among a clump of students. Randall felt their eyes on him.

"Lookin' good, Randall," said Paul Lunde. Randall felt the boy's nearness right behind him. He ducked his head and moved into the corner by the door.

Where was the invisible wall that followed him like a force field wherever he went?

Suddenly Randall was shaking. He didn't know why he was shaking but he couldn't make it stop. He couldn't fasten his mind on to anything solid. Strange shapes and pale colors flitted and faded where his dreaming usually was. A cracking and crumbling he could almost hear surged around his heart. Nothing would stay still long enough for him to lean against or hold on to.

In his mind, Jean's eyes floated and faded; his Uncle Luke rode off; his mother rocked herself back and forth, one hand covering her mouth. "What are those? Bites on your arms?" asked Victoria. Was that a bell ringing? Or was it a bell his mind remembered?

"Move it, Randall." Paul Lunde pushed past him with two other boys. As if watching some disjointed nightmare, Randall cringed against the wall while three other students pushed past him through the left door—*his* door. Their clothes brushed against him. He could feel the warmth from their energy and he stifled a cry. Inside, the boys joined the herd of students going through the right door.

Randall waited until they were all on their way down the hall. Then he slowly opened his door. In a daze he stumbled to his classroom, no longer trying to control the trembling or quiet the sound of his heart cracking. He moved like a drowning person through the clutter of chattering students to the back of the room.

His desk was like an island in a wild sea. And inside his desk he knew something solid waited, a lifesaver—his big, old notebook. He could feel his heart quieting down, the trembling lessened. He sat down gratefully and opened his desk. There were his crayons, worn and familiar. There were his pencils and his pen, his felt tips. But the big notebook with the faded cloth cover was gone.

From a long way off Randall heard a stifled wail. Something was falling—falling. *To the forest floor— long legs buckling.* In the distance, someone yelled, "It's Randall, Ms. Birchwood! Randall fell out of his seat!"

Randall dreamed. He dreamed himself drawing. The picnic table, with tree shadows crosshatched across its surface, kept shrinking under his pencil. He stabbed it with the lead and the fried chicken shook in its dish, but the table finally stayed still.

Then Randall attacked the problem of light spreading out from the lake water, the faint lambent glow behind faces of smiling strangers. But the smiles faded; the faces disappeared. Faceless bodies, gathered around the table, whispered and whispered.

He opened his notebook to hide—but all his drawings had faded or run as if they'd been given a bath.

Several thoughts flew in and out of Ms. Birchwood's mind as she hurried to the back of the classroom where a knot of students was clustered near Randall Lord's desk.

It's some kind of joke, was the first thought. But it was the kind of joke only Paul Lunde with his happy spirit or devilish Mike Spellman would pull—not Randall Lord. Randall never fell out of his desk seat for laughs. Her next thought hit the mark.

"Oh, no—the notebook," she said, half aloud. "I should have left the notebook there." As soon as she said that, she dismissed it as farfetched. "I'm just feeling guilty," she thought.

At that moment, Randall Lord's notebook was sitting on the principal's desk. Ms. Birchwood had taken it to Mr. Needem in the hopes that it would startle him into some kind of action. Mr. Needem wasn't in his office. "Classroom emergency," said his secretary, Miss Wyeth. Mr. Needem was always out on an emergency.

Ms. Birchwood had left Randall's notebook

right in the middle of Mr. Needem's desk with a note.

> *Mr. Needem,*
> *These remarkable drawings were done by Randall Lord—free hand! He is self-taught. I think this school should nourish gifts like Randall's. Do you have any ideas?*

Ms. Birchwood herself had a few ideas, but she thought it wise to let Mr. Needem come to these conclusions by himself. If he didn't, then she could nudge him a little in the right direction. Maybe call in a social worker. Or an artist who could take Randall under his or her wing. The first step would be to see to it that Randall could stay clean.

But he didn't seem so dirty when she got to his desk. Even so, her students, except for Paul Lunde, hadn't gotten too close. Paul was kneeling on the floor near Randall's curled body.

"I think he took a bath," said Paul. "He smells good even."

Randall's profile stood out pale against the floor. His eyes were partway open. Ms. Birchwood knelt and felt his pulse. His wrist was clean; his pulse seemed normal. She slipped one arm under his body and gathered him up.

68

"Take his legs, Paul," she ordered. Together they propped Randall in his seat. Ms. Birchwood supported his head. He *did* smell clean.

"Someone go get a wet paper towel," she said. "You—Kendra—in the bathroom—cold water." She didn't correct Kendra when she ran from the room.

"Tiffany, go to Mr. Needem's office. Tell him or Miss Wyeth that Randall Lord has passed out. Quick now!"

"Can I run, Ms. Birchwood. Can I run?" cried Tiffany. "Kendra ran. Should I run?"

"Run!" hollered Ms. Birchwood. Tiffany took off.

Ms. Birchwood could feel Randall begin to support his own head. His eyes were flickering.

O where have you been, Lord Randal, my son? O where have you been, my handsome young man? Ms. Birchwood felt a wave of sorrow wash over her. *Mother mak my bed soon; I fain woud lie doun.*

"Randall," she said softly. The eyes flickered open and Ms. Birchwood found herself looking into the deep, purple-blue.

"Randall, would you like to put your head down on your desk for a bit? Or would you like to lie down in the first aid room?"

She couldn't read what was going on in his eyes.

"Would you like to go home?" Then she was both shocked and mystified by what he said.

"I want them back." His voice was thin but clear. "They're mine! I don't care if they're dirty. Don't you put them in the wastepaper basket! Don't give them a bath. I'll leave them at home. I'll leave them at home!"

Randall was resting, lying on the lumpy cot in the first aid room next to Mr. Needem's office. He felt more tired than he'd ever felt before. Ms. Birchwood had put a thin blanket over him that warmed him and had softened the shakiness away. His body seemed to melt into the warmth.

The little room was dimly lit and smelled of coffee. Mr. Needem came in to pour himself a cup. He stopped by the cot and smiled at Randall. Mr. Needem had never smiled at Randall before.

"How's our artist doing?" he asked jovially. Then Mr. Needem leaned over and peered into Randall's face. His expression was puzzled.

"Guess you'll live, Randall," he joked. "Ms. Birchwood claims you're suffering from stress. At your age. Isn't that something?"

Randall opened his mouth to ask Mr. Needem a

question, but Mr. Needem's attention was pulled away by the crackling of the paging microphone and Miss Wyeth's voice calling him.

"See ya later, pal," he said and left before Randall could ask him if Parents' Day had started. Had parents come? Had Uncle Luke come? He started to raise himself up, but the coziness of the cot was too good to leave. He sank back down. "How's our artist doing?" His eyes closed. His hands uncurled; his lips parted. Randall slept.

"I knew I should have gone to school instead of spending the entire morning at the dentist," wailed Jean. She was sitting at the big round kitchen table doing her homework. Her mother had just finished washing her hair in the yellow bathroom and now sat opposite Jean with one of the thick yellow towels.

"I *knew* I should have gone to school."

"Do your math," said Jean's mother. She began to dry her head of raging, wet, curly hair.

"What's more important?" insisted Jean indignantly. "Math? Or a human being?"

"Do your math, Jean," said her mother.

"I mean Randall needed me there. It was his first

clean day at school. Somebody might have made fun of him." Jean began to work herself up into an angry froth. "Somebody could have called him a name. I could have punched them out."

"Do your math," repeated Jean's mother, who was now dragging a big-toothed comb through her wet mop.

"I hate math," sulked Jean.

"I hate my hair," said Jean's mother, leaning back and shaking out her hair behind her.

"It shrinks when it's wet," said Jean.

"My hair or your math brain?" asked her mother.

"Do your hair," ordered Jean in her mother's voice and they both began to giggle.

Later on, after Jean had struggled through ten math problems, she asked her father, "Why would Randall pass out, Dad? He looked worn out when I sneaked into the first aid room. He thought it was Parents' Day—and Parents' Day isn't till tomorrow. He told me that the bath made him sick. Baths don't make you sick. Ms. Birchwood said he doesn't get good food. The other kids think it's because he stopped wearing Mike Spellman's brother's jacket."

"I don't think it was the bath itself, Jean," said

her father. "And Randall probably is undernourished. But I think it might have been the change. Randall most likely didn't feel sweet and clean like you do after a bath. He probably felt naked and scared. Being dirty might have been like a shield to Randall."

"That's pretty hard to imagine," said Jean. Naked was one thing; clean was another. But, she thought, it was true that, clean, Randall had looked kind of defenseless.

"I wonder what he's having for dinner tonight," she said. "I mean we're having pork steaks and homemade sauerkraut and noodles, and green beans from last year's garden. I wonder what Randall's eating tonight. I wonder if his Uncle Luke will come to Parents' Day tomorrow. I wonder if Randall will feel better."

"You wonder too much, Jean," said her father. He was lifting his own special sauerkraut out of a big gray crock. "But that's probably a good thing," he added.

Randall was waiting. No other children waited with him at the school bus stop. It was a cloudy day, windy, too. He was wearing Mike Spellman's older brother's coat. He hadn't been going to wear it ever again but his mother had started to cry when he left the house in his shirtsleeves. Even so, Randall was shivering a little. He'd never been to school on Parents' Day. He was hoping his Uncle Luke would be there. Ms. Birchwood had said she would hang up his drawings. She had said they were good—wonderful, she had said. So had the principal. "How's our artist doing?" he had asked.

Randall was waiting. He hadn't washed very much. His clothes felt more comfortable now. But he didn't want the shakes to return so he hadn't washed too long under the pump. Jean had told him it wasn't the soap or the water or the bathtub that had given him the shakes, but Randall wasn't taking any chances.

He waited. Randall didn't know that the bus didn't run on Parents' Day.

Jean loved Parents' Day. She got to show off her father's debonair good looks. She got to ride to school in the jeep instead of the school bus. She got to show off *for* her handsome father. She was eager for him to see her desk and the trapeze trick she could do on the playground and Mike Spellman's broken arm with all the writing on the cast.

She would show him her four 100 percent spelling tests on the wall and her poem about the dead bird. She hoped that Kendra would cooperate and they could perform for him the dance they were rehearsing for the fifth-grade variety show.

She knew her dad had to spend some time discussing her, Jean, with Ms. Birchwood, and maybe looking around the room. She knew he'd probably chat with other parents—mostly mothers—and he would shake hands with Mr. Needem. She could mess around on the playground with the other kids who came on Parents' Day while he did the boring adult stuff.

Parents' Day was a great day to be at school. Not all parents brought their kids with them and there was no schoolwork to do. You could just show off and play with the kids that came.

Jean hoped Randall would be there so she could show him off maybe. Or show off her dad to Randall. "He makes a *mean* sauerkraut," she might tell Randall.

She didn't quite know what she'd tell her dad about Randall. "Here's the dirty kid we were discussing Monday night." Or, "Meet Randall. You think *my* tub rings are bad." Or, "Meet Randall. His hair's growing back."

She didn't quite know what to tell her father

about Randall until she got to her classroom. Just outside the door she was met by her own face! Posted in the hallway for everyone to see was a pencil drawing of her face with only the eyes colored in—a dark, wet-looking hazel. It made all the other drawings posted there really look like kid drawings.

Before she could say a word, her father exclaimed, "Jean! Who did this?" He got up really close and examined it as if for invisible ink. Then he stood way back. "Wait till your mother sees this! Wonder if the artist will sell? When did he come to the school? Who did it?"

Even if she hadn't seen the caption on a separate slip beneath the nicely matted drawing, Jean would have known.

"My friend Randall did it," she said, barely able to keep the surprise and joy out of her voice.

It had started to rain. The school bus had not come and Randall wondered if he had missed it. He began to walk. The rain was light and, instead of deepening his shivers, seemed to smooth them out. But Randall despaired. It would take him a long time to get to school walking the six miles. An hour and a half? Two hours? He had never walked the whole way before. How would Uncle Luke find his room? How would he know Ms. Birchwood? Would he wait for Randall?

Randall began to run in the lightly falling rain. Slowly the ground beneath his feet dampened, then turned to mud. Every once in a while he slowed down and walked, gasping for breath. Then he started running again.

There were a few kids playing in the playground at school when Luke Meriweather roared into the schoolyard on the 650, one leg balanced out to steady his stop.

All the kids stopped to stare at the motorcycle. Then they sized up the man, lean and taut as a teenager but with old eyes, fine wrinkles around them.

The man looked a little bit like Randall, the same burned-butter hair, the same look to his face, delicate but strong. He looked shy, too. He wasn't dirty but everyone in the playground knew that this had to be Randall's Uncle Luke.

Paul Lunde sauntered over, eyeing the 650. "What a beaut," he said to Luke. Then he added,

"Randall's not here. He passed out yesterday in class."

Oh geez, Tom Lord's home, was Luke's first thought. But he knew Tom Lord couldn't be home. He was in jail. And he'd be there for a good long time, for attempted murder. Luke had found out the other night at the bar that Tom Lord had just about killed some gal over in Birch County. Beat her senseless and left her on the floor of her kitchen.

"Yeah," said some other kids, clustering around the tall, wiry man and his motorcycle. "Randall *fainted*."

"Better get on over to Veery," thought Luke.

"Wait!" someone yelled, and he saw a girl running toward him.

"Are you Uncle Luke?" she gasped. She had dark, straight hair and big, serious eyes.

"I'm Randall's friend, Jean. You should come into the classroom before you leave. You should have a conference with Ms. Birchwood. You should *see* what Randall's done. You won't believe it!"

The rain was heavier now and, despite Mike Spellman's brother's coat, Randall was soaked to the skin. Cars passed on the road and he no longer avoided being splashed. He worried. Motorcycles could have accidents in rain, skidding and sliding.

A silver car passed, then slowed, stopped, and began to back up. On the back bumper was a "You Gotta Have Art" sticker. It was Jean's mother. Mrs. Neary leaned over and opened the passenger door.

"Randall? Is that you? What're you doing out here?"

"I missed the bus," said Randall hopefully.

"Well, get on in. Here, sit on Mr. Neary's raincoat. You're sopping." She dragged a raincoat from the back and spread it over the seat. "There's no bus today. Parents bring their kids."

Randall's despair returned. What was he bothering for? Why go to school? Luke wouldn't be there.

"I'm going to the school. Mr. Neary just called and suggested I pop over. Said there was something there I ought to see. Do you have any idea what it could be?"

Randall thought. "Jean got four A's on her spelling. She's got a poem put up in the hall about a dead bird."

"No," said Jean's mother. "I've seen those. No, he said I had to see it to believe it. He said it was a special treat and I could do something about it."

Randall suspected that Mrs. Neary liked things she could do something about. But he had no idea what it could be.

Jean Worth Neary began jumping up and down when her mother's car pulled into the schoolyard. It had stopped raining and most of the students were standing around in the yard. When a very wet Randall got out of the car, Jean's eyes went big. Then she glared at her mother.

"You should have let him dry off, at least. We've got lots of towels. You should have let him wear Moriah's Calvins, at least. And one of my T's."

Mrs. Neary laughed a big, delighted laugh. "Jean. Randall didn't take a bath, honey. I found him walking to school in the rain."

Jean looked at Randall.

"Rain can't hurt you," he said.

"Yeah. Right," said Jean, calming down. "Right. It's just another kind of bath. But you're sopping. And your Uncle Luke's here. He's talking with Ms. Birchwood."

All of Randall's life he would remember the soaring feeling that swept through him then. It almost had a sound, a kind of sweet music. He

stood trapped inside the music between a gravelly
puddle and his friend, Jean.

Randall felt hot and lightheaded and so hopeful
he thought his head would explode. He and Jean
stood just inside the door of his classroom. There
by Ms. Birchwood's desk were the powerful, real
people in his life. They were looking at his drawings on the desk. They were saying things about
him. He heard fragments of their voices—Luke
muttering, "His momma used to draw flowers. . . ." Mrs. Neary talking about scholarships at
the museum. "I'd like my committee to see
these." Mr. Neary held the drawing of Jean
jumping rope, his hands delicate and careful. Ms.
Birchwood was displaying the deer with the red
heart.

"Singapore," said Randall into the room. He said
it quietly and Jean, beside him, said, "Huh?"

The four grown people turned around, Ms.
Birchwood, Jean's mother and father, his Uncle
Luke. They all smiled at him, pleased he was
there.

"It was really cool," said Jean, "when Uncle Luke shook Randall's hand. I mean I'd expect some sort of hug."

The rain had started up again as Jean and her father were driving back home in the jeep.

"I'd *insist* on a hug," she added. "But that was really cool."

"Your friend Randall is a very talented boy," said Jean's father. "Your mother's sure she can get him a scholarship at the museum. She thinks she can get the Rotary Club to raise some money to help the family out, too. Rotary people like to do good deeds, more specifically, deeds that are clear cut and heartwarming."

"Good," said Jean, "Randall can use all the warmth he can get."

"Your mother also thinks Randall should go right into an adult class at the museum. She says he doesn't even need beginning drawing, that he's well past that."

"Wow," said Jean. "He had that stuff in his desk all this time and nobody knew. I mean *I* didn't know and none of the other kids knew. I can't wait to see some of their faces tomorrow when they see Randall's drawings plastered all over the place."

"I can't wait to hear what your mother's scholarship committee says when they find out Randall's age," said her dad.

"Mr. Needem says that in America anyone can be anything they want," speculated Jean. "I mean Randall could be president of the United States!"

She thought a moment, then shook her head. "No, that's not his style. That's more my style. Actually, the Secret Service is more my style."

"Well, Jean," said her father wryly, "if your mother doesn't make it as the first woman president, you probably will."

"Then Randall could be the First Gentleman," said Jean, squeezing out a giggle. "And redecorate the White House."

Randall was dreaming. He sat in the back of the truck among the upturned legs of chairs and a table. The wind stirred the burned-butter top of his newly grown hair. The truck rattled down the late afternoon highway. His Uncle Luke had traded his motorcycle for this solid, old truck. It had made Randall sad at first but Luke had said, "Family needs a truck, not a motorcycle."

Randall's mother would go to a dentist now as soon as they could all talk her into it. Luke had said to her, "Veery, you used to smile so sweet when we were kids. Your skin's forgot the feel of a smile. We're gonna get you all fixed up."

Randall couldn't remember his mother smiling. But he had drawn a picture of her wearing a pretty smile to give her the idea.

Randall was sitting on a manila envelope that contained ten stamped envelopes with Jean's name and address. He wouldn't be going to the same school with her until junior high. But maybe he'd see her when he went to the museum on Saturday for art class. The manila envelope also contained a baby picture of Jean. "The only sexy picture of me has Moriah in it, too, and she looks sexier," Jean had told him.

Randall took the picture out and tried to find the Jean he knew in the baby picture. The baby had a joyous smile and a fat, round chin. The eyes were the same—big and shining—but it was the eagerness he finally recognized. He carefully put the picture back into the manila envelope.

Then Randall dreamed of the new house they were headed for. It had a yard and grass that had to be mowed. It had a washing machine in its own room. Randall would have to share a bedroom with Toby and Jacob, but he made them quiet and sleeping in the dream. He put them in their own beds on yellow sheets so clean. He put Jean's baby picture on the wall by his bed. Then he dreamed of Jean's face as it looked when she handed him the manila envelope.

"Don't feel bad about deserting me," she had told him. Then she added, "I think the Rotary people are going to do something heartwarming for your family." Her large eyes were rounder and glossier than usual.

"Remember—you have to write," she growled.

"I will," said Randall.

Then, his voice jiggled by the motion of the truck, he said it again. Then he shouted back at the receding road, his voice spinning into the air, carried by the wind back to where he'd been.

Shouting, "I will! I will!"

ABOUT THE AUTHOR

CAROL FENNER lives in Battle Creek, Michigan. She has written seven books for young readers, and she has also found time to travel around Michigan and nearby states, speaking and conducting workshops under such programs as the Michigan Council for the Arts' Creative Writers in Schools. It was during one of those school visits that Carol Fenner found the boy who has become Randall in her story.

THE BEST OF SKYLARK